FALL IS MURDER

SERIES BY NELLIE H. STEELE

Cate Kensie Mysteries

Shadow Slayers Stories

Lily & Cassie by the Sea Mysteries

Pearl Party Mysteries

Middle Age is Murder Cozy Mysteries

Duchess of Blackmoore Mysteries

Maggie Edwards Adventures

Clif & Ri on the Sea Adventures

Shelving Magic

FALL IS MURDER

A SALEM FALLS B&B PARANORMAL COZY MYSTERY

MIDDLE AGE IS MURDER COZY MYSTERIES
BOOK 2.5

NELLIE H. STEELE

This is a work of fiction. Names, characters, places, and incidents either are the product of the author's imagination or are used fictitiously. Any resemblance to actual persons, living or dead, events, or locales is entirely coincidental.

Cover design by Stephanie A. Sovak.

Created with Vellum

CHAPTER 1

Lightning streaked through the sky, and rain pattered against the windows of the sprawling Victorian house. Ellie peered at the dark clouds. They seemed to be stuck over the tiny town of Salem Falls. Another rumble of thunder growled as she tugged the sheets from the bed and dumped them in the laundry basket.

Lola, her miniature bulldog, lifted her head as the thunder boomed, offering a growl.

"It's just a storm, Lola," Ellie said.

"I don't like it. It's too loud," the dog answered.

"I know you don't like it, but it's okay. Why don't you go take a nap in the bedroom? It won't be as loud there."

Lola's dark brown eyes studied her. "What if you need me?"

"I'm just doing laundry. I'll be fine."

"You never know what could happen," Lola answered.

"Tell you what. I just need to throw these in the wash, then we'll curl up together with a movie."

Cleo stalked into the room, shaking her tail. "You making popcorn? It's the least you can do."

Ellie hefted the basket onto her hip and stared at the black cat across the room. "Least I can do? What's that mean?"

"For subjecting us to this weather," Cleo shot back as they trailed behind Ellie down to the laundry room.

"I didn't subject you to it! I can't help that it's raining."

Lola craned her neck to stare up at Ellie as she loaded the washer. "But since it is, we should have popcorn."

"Fine. Why don't you two go pick a movie, and I'll make the popcorn?"

"How do you expect us to do that?" Cleo asked. "I can't work the TV."

"Yes, you can. You turn it on in the middle of the night all the time."

"By accident. I accidentally walk on it."

Ellie slammed the lid shut and set a hand on her hip. "Oh, really? By sheer chance? Yeah, right. Because you *happen* to do it whenever you want my attention."

"Not true. I figure while you're up, though, there's time for a quick chat."

"Whatever," Ellie said.

Lola ducked as lightning flashed outside.

"Just head up and pick out your spots."

"I call the middle of the bed!" Cleo called as she raced from the kitchen. Lola clopped after her.

Ellie shook her head as she filled her glass popcorn maker with kernels. "Those two. How did I get so lucky to have hit my head and woken up to talking pets?"

With the popcorn button pressed, Ellie crossed her arms, suppressing a shiver as the storm continued to rage outside. Rain pounded against the roof as the glass container spun inside the microwave.

The long beep of the microwave drew her attention back to her food. She pulled open the door and emptied the delicious-smelling treat into a large bowl. With a dash of salt sprinkled on top, she headed upstairs.

Voices floated from the bedroom at the top of the stairs. "Move over," Cleo's sassy voice said.

"I'll fall off the bed."

"So? You're a dog, you belong on the floor."

"That's not true."

"Enough, girls," Ellie said as she strode into the room. "Just for that, I'm going to put the popcorn way up here and change into my jammies first."

"It'll get cold!" Cleo cried.

"Oh, darn," Ellie said as she stuck the bowl on a high dresser across the room and shimmied out of her pants. Within minutes, she pulled her fluffy robe around her and snugged the belt tighter. "Now, move over, both of you."

She retrieved the popcorn bowl before she tossed back the covers and shooed the animals over.

"I picked my spot," Cleo said, her ears flattened against her head as she fought to keep her place in the middle of the bed.

Ellie tossed a piece of popcorn to the side. Cleo dove for it, and Ellie took full advantage, shimmying further under the covers.

"Hey!" Cleo shouted as she found Ellie's knees in her former spot.

Ellie grinned at her as she grabbed the remote and popped a piece of popcorn into her mouth. She patted the spot formed by the crook of her knees. Lola raced over to curl into it, squeezing her squat body into the space and setting her chin on Ellie's shin.

Cleo shook a paw and glanced at Ellie. "Now what, smarty?"

Ellie pulled a pillow against her side and patted it. "Here you go. A nice, cushy pillow for you."

Cleo stared at it for a moment, then sauntered over. "Fine, but only because this is one of the orthopedic kind. It's good for my back."

"That's why I picked it," Ellie said, flicking on the television across the room.

Thunder rumbled again outside, and the rain intensified as she navigated the selection.

Cleo licked a paw. "Pick something good. Not one of those weird women movies."

Ellie wrinkled her brow as she scrolled through the recommended movies. "What's that supposed to mean?"

"You know...Ellie gets a divorce but wants to start her life fresh. She finds new friends and new challenges in a small town."

"You just literally summarized my life."

"Yeah, boring. Pick something else. Something like...Ellie gets a divorce, but she snaps and kills her ex-husband..."

"No," Ellie said.

"No murder movies," Lola echoed.

Ellie offered the dog another piece of popcorn before she clicked on a movie and read the synopsis. "How's this? A college professor and her dog–"

"No dog movies," Cleo said.

"All right," Ellie said, trying the next one. "A mother and daughter move to a small seaside town. Together with their one-eyed cat–"

"What?!" Cleo exclaimed. "One-eyed?"

"No cats," Lola said.

Cleo narrowed her eyes at the dog. "Why, Butterball?"

"If we can't watch dogs, then we can't watch cats."

"Well said, Lola. That leaves us with these two on our list. Two unsuspecting sisters become trapped at a mansion during a storm when a murder occurs–"

"No murders!" Lola repeated.

"Oh, right. Okay, this one it is," Ellie clicked to select the last movie.

"What's it about?" Cleo asked.

"A young woman experiences terrifying nightmares and must discover the secrets lurking in the shadows of her past before they destroy her and the world."

Cleo nestled in and stared at the screen. "Oh, yeah. World-ending stuff is my favorite. Let's hope she doesn't succeed."

"Don't say that," Ellie said, snuggling into her pillows and reaching for more popcorn as the opening scenes played on the screen.

A terrified woman gasped for breath as she raced through a dark cave. Thunder rumbled outside, adding ambience to the scary scene.

"Run, lady! Somebody's chasing you!" Cleo shouted. "Run for your life!"

"Who is chasing her, Ellie?" Lola asked, her eyes transfixed as the blonde's hair blew behind her.

"I don't know."

"Why is she being chased?"

"I don't know." Ellie shrugged as she grabbed another handful of popcorn.

On-screen, the woman startled awake, gasping for breath.

Lola wagged her tail as the woman swung her legs over the side of the bed. "Why is she having nightmares?"

"Lola, I don't know. I didn't get the script ahead of time."

"Why not?" Cleo asked. "Would have been useful to shut the dummy dog up."

Ellie clicked her tongue and aimed the remote at the TV, pressing the volume button repeatedly. "Pipe down, you two. Just watch the movie."

A loud crack of thunder drew Lola's attention to the

window. Her wrinkled face scrunched even more before she glanced at Ellie.

"It's fine," Ellie said. "Just a storm."

"Sounds bad," she said, with a wag of her tail.

"Yeah," Cleo added, "I've never heard a storm this bad here."

"Really? In all the years you've been here, it's never stormed like this?"

"Not like this," Lola answered, fixing her gaze on the window again.

Cleo batted her tail as lightning flashed again. "Nope. Worst storm I've ever lived through."

Ellie's phone chimed, and she swiped it from the charging pad. A new message from her best friend, Mia, appeared on the lock screen: *You riding out the storm okay?*

She typed back: *So far, so good.*

She tossed the phone to the side, with a sigh. "Now, I missed what happened."

"A hot guy left a package on her porch," Cleo reported.

"A hot guy?" Ellie asked as her phone beeped again.

"Yeah. Real looker. I bet he's evil."

"That's not a given." Ellie swiped open her message and read Mia's latest text: *Rickie said there's a tornado warning. I'm heading over.*

Ellie frowned at both parts of the message as her fingers flew across the virtual keyboard. *Tornado warning? Stay put! Don't go out! I'm fine.*

"You're missing it again," Cleo said. "He gave her a music box. I bet it's cursed."

"Do you think all good looking people are evil?"

"Of course not. I'm beautiful and not evil. Nathan is handsome and not evil."

"Oh, right. I forgot you have the hots for the deputy."

She swiped into her phone again and read the latest: *I'm*

already here. On the porch. What did you lock the door for?

"Ugh," Ellie groaned as she struggled to free herself and crawl out of her nest.

"Where are you going?" Cleo asked.

"Mia's here."

"Tell her to leave," Cleo said as Lola leapt from the bed to follow Ellie as she hurried from the room, tugging her robe tighter around her.

She pounded down the stairs, crossed to the door, unlocked and pulled it open. Rain pelted the ground outside and dripped from the porch roof.

Mia hefted her bag from the porch to her shoulder as she grinned at Ellie. "You don't happen to have a room for rent, do you?"

Ellie rolled her eyes despite the corners of her lips turning up. "Get in here. You shouldn't be out in this storm, though."

"I hopped into my car the moment Rick texted. It's way better to be here with you than at my apartment anyway." Mia flicked her blonde braid over her shoulder as she stepped into the foyer.

Ellie pressed the door closed against the fierce wind and locked it. "We're watching a movie upstairs. I've got popcorn."

"Ohhh, what movie?" Mia asked as she climbed the stairs behind Ellie and Lola.

"*Shadows of the Past,*" Ellie answered.

"Oh, pause it! I've been wanting to see it."

"I'll do you one better. We'll restart it. I've missed half of it between Lola's fear of the storm and your texts."

"Thank goodness I was texting you!" Mia called over her shoulder as she hustled down the hall to her normal room. "I won't be long."

"Take your time," Ellie answered, stepping into her

bedroom. She crossed to the bed, grabbed the remote, and stopped the movie.

"Hey, we were watching that!" Cleo exclaimed.

"Yeah, and now we're not. We're waiting for Mia, and then we're going to start it over."

"Boring," Cleo said, with a flick of her paw.

"Well, I missed half of it," Ellie complained.

"So?"

"So, I have the opposable thumbs, and I control the remote."

Mia shuffled into the room in her fluffy robe and slippers. "Okay, ready. Move over, kitty, I'm coming in."

"You're kidding me," Cleo groaned as Mia bounced onto the bed. The cat pressed her ears back against her head as she scurried to find a new spot.

Lola rose to her feet and wagged her tail. "Hi, Mia."

"Hey, girl," Mia said, oblivious to the animal's voices.

After getting a pat on the head, Lola settled down to lay between the women. She snapped her head toward the window as thunder boomed again.

"It's okay, Lola. Just a storm. Nothing to worry about."

The wrinkly dog stared at Ellie. "I have a bad feeling, Ellie."

Ellie pointed the remote at the television and restarted the movie. The blonde raced through the cave.

Mia dug into the popcorn bowl as she slouched down, nestling into the pillows. A moment later, the room plunged into darkness. Lola lifted her head, her eyes wide as the lights came back on and the movie started again.

"Just a little atmosphere," Mia said.

"I don't mind if they'd stay off. I could finally get some sleep. Right after another piece of popcorn." Cleo reached her paw toward the bowl.

"Here you go, Kitty," Mia said, tossing a piece onto the

duvet for Cleo.

Lightning tore through the sky again as the winds picked up.

"It's really getting bad out there."

Mia glanced at her phone screen as she tossed another piece of popcorn into her mouth. "Mmm-hmm. Rickie just texted and said they have trees down everywhere. A few people on the west side of town are out of power."

"Ugh, that stinks."

Mia bobbed her head up and down as she tossed her phone to the side and grabbed another handful of popcorn. "I should have brought candy."

"I've got some downstairs. I always keep chocolate in the house."

Mia swung her legs over the edge of the bed, but Ellie waved her back. "I've got it. Just give me a minute to run downstairs."

She paused the movie and pushed off the bed. With her slippers on, she shambled across the room and into the hall.

Lola's nails clopped across the floor after she leapt down from the bed. "I'll come, too, Ellie."

"I didn't need your help, Lola. You should have stayed asleep."

Ellie twisted to glance at the dog as she lowered her foot to the first step. The lights flickered on and off after a massive boom of thunder. Ellie startled, losing her footing.

She grasped at the railing in a desperate attempt to stay upright, but she slipped, sliding down to the landing and smacking her head on the step.

"ELLIE!" Lola shouted while racing down the stairs.

Stars danced in front of her. "Ow."

Her eyelids grew heavy, and she let her head fall back against the hard stair while the world faded to black around her.

CHAPTER 2

Muffled voices mumbled in the distance. A cool rag pressed against her forehead.

Ellie twitched, squirming with her eyes still closed. A second later, her eyelids fluttered open. She lay on her bed. The dog next to her leapt to her feet. A black, furry face leaned over her.

"She's alive!" Cleo's voice said.

Lola's tail wagged as Ellie tried to push up to her elbows.

"Oh, easy there, don't be a Dumb Dora," Mia said.

Ellie screwed up her face. "What? Why are you talking like that?"

"Talking like what?" she asked, adjusting her robe.

Ellie studied it. It didn't look anything like the one she was wearing when she came in earlier.

Thunder rumbled overhead as Ellie tried to push up to sit again. "I'm fine. My head doesn't even hurt."

"There's no need for all that," Mia said, pushing her back into the pillows. "Everything's Jake. Let's just wait for the doc. Although, in this storm, he may be a bit late."

"Doctor? Mia, I think you're the one who needs a doctor. Why are you using that ridiculous slang?"

"Ridiculous slang? And who is Mia?"

Ellie stared at the woman in front of her. "You are."

"Says you!" she responded. "What kind of nonsense is this? I think you may have hit your head harder than I realized."

Ellie slid her eyes shut and collapsed back into the pillows. "Honestly, Mia, I'm really not in the mood for this."

"Please stop calling me 'Mia.' That's not my name."

Ellie rubbed her temples as a dull ache built in them. "All right, fine. What's your name? Oh, please don't say 'Cookie.' I'm *not* calling you the pet name Rick uses for you."

Mia leapt to her feet and paced around the floor. "I'm really confused by your behavior. Are you loose from the looney bin?"

"No." Ellie sighed and shook her head. "What is going on here?"

"What is going on here is, I heard a loud thud. When I went out of my room, I found you collapsed on the landing. Where you came from, I don't know! But there you were. I assume you're the new boarder?"

"New boarder?" Ellie's mind spun with the conversation. Was this some sort of joke? It wasn't funny. Especially with her headache.

"Yes. I didn't let you in earlier, but I was out. Maybe someone else did. I had a new girl coming. Are you her? What's your name?"

"Ellie," she answered instinctively before flinging her hands down at her sides. "Mia, look, I have a headache. I'd just like some aspirin and a warm compress. Not this weird game."

"Ellie," Mia said, tapping her lips with a finger, "mmm, no. Elizabeth. Elizabeth was supposed to come in today."

Ellie heaved a sigh. "Okay, fine. I'll play. What's your name?"

The woman raised her chin and smiled at Ellie. "I'm Doris Dixon. And I own this joint."

"Doris Dixon?"

"Mmm-hmm."

Ellie scrunched her features. "Is this some kind of weird flirting thing with Rick?"

"Who is Rick?"

Ellie let her head fall back against the pillow. "You know what, never mind. Where's my phone? I'll call him and ask."

"The telephone? Just had that installed. Can you believe this place didn't come with one already? What century is this?"

"Same question I have." Ellie searched the nightstand next to her. She pinched her eyebrows together as she found it devoid of any of her possessions. "Hey! What happened to all my stuff?"

She glanced at the lamp, realizing it looked nothing like hers.

"Sorry, Doll, but this is my room. If you want to stay, I do have an open spot, but it's at the end of the hall. But it's five dollars a week, eighteen if you want to pay for the month upfront. That includes room and board and your meals. But you are responsible for keeping your room tidy, and we all pitch in to clean the common areas on Saturday mornings."

Ellie drummed her fingers on the bed as she glanced at the pets next to her. "All right, fine. I'll stay. Now, where's my phone?"

"Downstairs on the foyer table."

"Okay," Ellie grunted as she swung her legs over the side of the bed and pushed herself to stand. She shuffled from the room to the stairs, shaking her head. "Ridiculous."

She lumbered down the stairs. Her head pounded with

every step. She rubbed at her forehead as she stepped on the hardwood floor and swung around the railing to the table.

Her eyes went wide as she stared down at the old-fashioned phone on the antique table. She glanced into the sitting room and screwed up her face. The furniture was completely different.

The only thing that looked the same in the space was the grandfather clock. How had they pulled this off? It would have required hours to redecorate at least.

She shuffled to the phone and picked up the receiver. A curt voice answered, "What number please?"

"Uh…" She hesitated. What number did she want to call? "Sheriff's Office. Salem Falls Sheriff's Office."

"One moment please."

Ellie tapped her foot on the floor as she waited for the line to connect. What the heck was going on here?

A female voice answered on the other end of the line. "Salem Falls Sheriff's Office."

"Hazel, thank goodness. Is Rick there?"

"Who?"

"Rick. Sheriff Rick. Is Sheriff Rick there?"

"Uh…the sheriff is here. Ummm, let me connect you."

A noise sounded on the opposite end as the woman shouted. "Sheriff! Call for you…I don't know."

A commotion sounded before a new voice came on the line. "Salem Falls Sheriff here. What can I do for you?"

Ellie's features twisted. "Mac?"

"No. This is Sheriff Chester West. Can I help you?"

"Chester? What happened to Rick?"

"Who?" he asked.

"Look, Mac, it's Ellie. What's going on here?"

"I don't know an Ellie. You all right, lady?"

Mia tapped her on the shoulder before signaling for her to hand over the phone. "Hi, Chester. Doris here…uh huh…

that's right. Yes, with the big clap of thunder. Uh huh. I'd appreciate that. You're a pal."

She replaced the receiver and slid the phone onto the table.

Ellie massaged her temples. "What is going on here?"

"Maybe you should sit down, Doll."

A whiny siren sounding like it belonged in an old movie cut through the air as Mia guided Ellie into the living room. She plopped on the couch, rubbing at it as though it wasn't real.

"I'll get you some water."

Lola loped down the stairs and wagged her tail at Ellie. "Please tell me this is all some kind of joke?"

"This is all some kind of joke," the dog answered.

"Thank goodness."

"Except it's not," Cleo said with a shake of her head as she slinked around the corner.

"What? What do you mean, Cleo?"

"Why are you calling me by that ridiculous name? My name is Kitty."

"Kitty?" Ellie exclaimed, her fingers wrapping around the edge of the pillow and squeezing. "You *hate* being called Kitty. Mia calls you Kitty all the time, and you hate it."

"Why would I hate it? It's my name. And who is Mia?"

"Mia. The blonde bringing me the water."

"Doris?" Cleo asked.

Ellie shook her head before she let it fall into her palm. She flicked her gaze to Lola. "I suppose you have a new name, too."

"No, my name is the same as it's always been. Mopsie."

"Mopsie?" Ellie slouched backward and slumped down the cushion.

The dog's tail wagged as Mia returned with the water.

Ellie gulped it down and wiped her lips with the back of her hand. "Something strange is going on here."

A knock sounded at the door, and Mia shuffled to it to answer it.

"Come on in, Sheriff." She stepped back and motioned for him to enter.

Ellie sat up straighter, expecting Rick to walk through the door. Instead, Mac appeared in what looked like an old-fashioned police uniform.

"Mac?" Ellie asked.

"Hi," the man said as he thrust out his hand. "I'm Chester. I'm the sheriff here. Doris called and said she found you on the stairs, collapsed."

"Uh, no, I own..." Heat washed over her as her gaze shifted from Mac's face to Mia's, then to the pets. "I...I'm..."

"Are you okay, Doll?"

Ellie rose to stand as her head swam. Her jaw flexed as she gritted her teeth. She hurried through the opening between the living room and dining room, passing through it into the kitchen.

None of the usual appliances were there. Everything looked ancient. She spun in search of anything familiar. As she twisted, she spotted a calendar hanging from a nail on the wall.

Red Xs crossed out the days. Her eyes went wide as she stared at the date. October 24, 1924.

"Nineteen twenty-four?!" she exclaimed. "No. No, it can't be."

Doris peeked in from the hall. Ellie shot her a panicked glance.

The blonde grabbed her by the shoulders and led her to the nearby table. She eased her into a chair. "Doc's on his way, Doll. You just sit down."

"Doctor?" Ellie questioned as she shot another quizzical glance at the calendar. "Is that calendar right?"

Doris patted her shoulder as she glanced at it. "Oops, what a silly goose I am. No! It's not right."

Ellie breathed a sigh of relief as she massaged her forehead. "Thank heavens."

"It's October twenty-sixth! I forgot to mark off the last two days." Doris grabbed her red marker and crossed off two more squares.

"Wait, what? It can't be right."

"Well, it is now, Doll."

"No. No, it can't be. It's not nineteen twenty-four. It can't be."

Chester wandered into the kitchen. "What year do you think it is?"

Ellie flicked her wide-eyed gaze between them. A lump formed in her throat as her knees went weak. If she wasn't sitting in the chair, she would have collapsed. She'd traveled back one hundred years into the past.

Tears formed in her eyes as she flicked her gaze to the two people eyeing her. "Not nineteen twenty-four."

Doris's features melted with concern as she eased into a chair across from Ellie and slid her arm across the table, grabbing her hand.

"Oh, Doll, what happened?"

Ellie shook her head. "One minute I was here…I was…"

She stopped talking. It was useless. How could she explain this? The answer came to her quickly. She couldn't. She had to be honest with them.

She'd likely end up locked in a crazy house. *What were asylums like in the nineteen twenties? Not nice places,* she concluded. She couldn't end up in a straitjacket.

Ellie leapt from her seat. "You know, I think I just need to lie down."

"Now, now, just a minute, young lady," Chester said, blocking the doorway. "I think you had better see our doc."

"Really, I don't need a doctor."

Doris rose and wrapped an arm around Ellie's shoulders. "He's already been called. Let me take you up to your room. We'll send him up when he gets here."

Ellie swallowed hard as random thoughts bombarded her mind. She shuffled forward and climbed the stairs in a haze. Mia led her down the hall past the room she had one hundred years from now before she opened the door at the end of the hall. The irony was not lost on Ellie that this was the room Mia occupied in her time.

She shook her head as she shuffled in and glanced around at the unfamiliar furniture. Tears burned her eyes.

"You just take a load off, Doll. The doc will be here any minute. And tell you what," Doris said, with a wave of her hand, "don't worry about the rent today. Let's just get you well."

Ellie swallowed the lump in her throat. She had no money. She couldn't pay for her room.

She spun to face the blonde, her features pinched. "Mia..." She squeezed her eyes closed and shook her head. "Doris, there's something I need to tell you."

"What is it, Doll?"

Ellie wrung her hands as she tried to think of the least crazy way to say what she needed to say. She glanced up into her friend's eyes. No, not her friend. A woman from 1924 named Doris. Could she trust her?

CHAPTER 3

"What is it, Ellie?" Doris asked again.

Ellie stared into her light blue eyes, her features pinching as she eased onto the bed. "I can't. You'll think I'm crazy."

"Well, that's just silly. Of course I won't. What is it?"

Footsteps shuffled down the hall, and voices floated to them. Chester appeared in the doorway with Andy.

"Andy?" Ellie murmured, her features scrunched as she stared at the grocer.

"Doc's here."

Andy pushed past Mac and entered the room. He set his black bag on the bed next to Ellie and popped it open. "Heard you took a little spill. How are you feeling?"

"F-fine," Ellie stammered as she stared up at him. Did she really want the local grocer to give her an exam?

He pulled a stethoscope from his bag and draped it around his neck. "Any dizziness? Blurred vision?"

"No."

"She has a little confusion," Chester said. "Of course, to be expected, given that the lady took a spill. But she was confused about the date."

Andy glanced at Chester and nodded before he slid a head mirror around his head. He approached Ellie and leaned closer to her.

She side-eyed him as he studied her.

"Where did you hit your head?"

"I don't know," she answered. "I don't remember."

"I see." He pressed the stethoscope against her pajama top. "Good."

"What do you remember?"

"Uhhh–" Ellie slid her eyes sideways to glance at him again, not wanting to answer his question.

"Can you tell me your name, hon?"

"Ellie."

"Do you have a last name?"

"Ellie Byrne."

"Good, Ellie." He pressed two fingers against her pulse point, while she resisted the urge to roll her eyes at his tone. She didn't like Andy in the present time, but as her patronizing doctor in the 1920s, she hated him. "Do you know where you're from? Are you married?"

"Not anymore. I'm from Winwick, but I moved to…I'm moving to Salem Falls."

"Not anymore? What does that mean? Are you widowed?"

Ellie began to shake her head when she stopped herself. "Yes. Yes, I am."

A divorcee in 1924 may not be accepted. She'd rather be a widow.

"Poor girl," Chester said, with a shake of his head. "Must have been a shock. You're not that old!"

"Right," Ellie said, with a nod. "A shock. That's why I'm a little mixed up. I guess it's taken more of a toll than I'd like to admit."

"Well, there's a cure for that," Andy said, patting her hand.

"There is?" Ellie asked.

He pulled his head mirror from his head and tossed it in his bag. "Absolutely. Bed rest. I'd rest for two days. Nothing too taxing. Maybe some light chores as tolerated. Don't overtax yourself, though, with reading or puzzles or anything difficult."

Ellie narrowed her eyes at the words. "Right."

"I'll recheck you in a few days. Until then, two aspirin before bed and a bit of leisure to help clear your head."

"Thanks, Doc. As always, a great assessment. I'll walk you out." Chester clapped the man on the back as he approached the door.

"We're still seeing each other for golf on Wednesday, right?" Andy asked as they disappeared into the hall.

"Poor dear," Doris said as she approached Ellie and fluffed her pillow. "Now, don't worry about a thing. We'll work out the details of your rent and chores when you're feeling better."

"I haven't got any money."

"Well, is it any wonder? Don't worry about that."

"But..."

Doris flicked her gaze to Ellie, a pillow still clutched in her hand. "What is it? You were about to tell me something before Dr. Jones came in. Was it about the money?"

Ellie began to nod when she squeezed her eyes closed. "No. You're going to think I'm nuts."

Doris plopped on the bed next to her and patted her hand. "What is it, Doll?"

Ellie licked her lips and flicked a sheepish gaze to her friend's look-alike. "When I fell..."

Doris raised her eyebrows and slid her head forward, prompting her to continue.

"I...I can't explain this, but...I'm not from nineteen

twenty-four."

Doris cocked her head. "What do you mean?"

"I mean...I'm...I came from the year twenty twenty-four." Ellie blew out a long breath. "There I said it. I'm not from nineteen twenty-four. I don't know how I got here. But I don't belong here. And I'm afraid I'll never get back."

Tears filled her eyes as she glanced down at her lap. In addition to being stuck here, she'd probably now be shoved into a nuthouse and kept there to live out the rest of her days.

"Oh, no," Doris pressed her palms to her cheeks as her jaw flapped open. "You're from the future?"

Ellie knitted her brow as she nodded. Did the woman believe her, or was she mocking her?

"Well, this is awful!"

"You believe me?" Ellie asked.

"Well, of course, Doll." Doris leapt from the bed and paced the floor in front of Ellie.

"That's a relief. I really thought you'd think I was crazy."

"Of course not. *The Time Machine* is my favorite book! I believe you."

Ellie blew out a sigh of relief. "Well, that's the first battle. Unfortunately, I think the second one is going to be much harder. How do I get home?"

Doris chewed her lower lip. "I may have an idea about that. But before we do anything, we need to get you some clothes. I think I'm about your size. Let me grab you some things."

Ellie flopped back on the bed as Doris flitted from the room. She covered her face with her hands before she sucked in a breath and wiped at her tear-stained cheeks.

"At least I'm not in an asylum."

Thank goodness for small blessings.

Before she could dwell on it further, Doris burst into the room with an armload of clothes. "Let's see what works."

After thirty minutes, they'd found two outfits that fit Ellie. She stared in the floor-length mirror at her drop-waist dress as she smoothed it over her.

"Thanks for these."

Doris kicked her legs in the air as she shifted off the edge of the bed. "Of course. We can't have you running around in your night things all over town!"

"I'm not so sure we should–"

"Of course we should, Doll! We've got to figure out a way to get you home. And I've got just the person to ask."

"Really?" Ellie asked.

Doris leapt to her feet, nodding and giggling. "This is so exciting! Come on."

"I'll be more excited when I'm back in the right time period."

Doris grabbed Ellie's hand and tugged her out the door and down the hall.

"There goes the Dumb Dora," Kitty said as they descended the stairs.

Ellie shot her a narrowed-eyed glance.

"What?" the cat shot back. "I can't help it nobody's home."

Mopsie wagged her tail as they passed. "We're home."

Kitty wrapped the dog across the head. "You're a dumb Dora, too."

"Ouch."

"Be back later, Mopsie and Kitty!" Doris called as she grabbed her purse and flung open the front door. "Stay out of trouble!"

They stepped into the brisk fall air.

Ellie tugged on her cloche hat with the matching tan and burgundy ribbon as they hurried down the stairs and ambled toward the road. "Where are we going?"

"To meet a gal who I think can help. She is brilliant!"

They reached the road, not paved in this era, and Doris veered to the left. Ellie paused, swinging her gaze the opposite way before she scurried to catch up. "She doesn't live in town?"

"No. She lives a bit further down the road. It's not far."

Ellie's sensible heels scraped against the dirt road as they continued under the autumn leaves. A cool breeze whipped past them, bowing the branches and sending a flurry of brightly colored foliage raining down around them.

Doris glanced behind her and winced. "We'd better hurry. Looks like another storm is blowing in."

Ellie shifted her gaze over her shoulder. Black clouds covered Salem Falls as another strong wind gust blew her skirt around and rustled her hair. She quickened her pace, pressing her hat against her head so it didn't blow off.

A few drops of rain pelted them as Doris veered off the road onto a gravel path. Ellie narrowed her eyes as she wobbled her way along the uneven terrain.

An overgrown metal gate prevented them from moving forward, flanked by two ivy-covered brick pillars.

Ellie's pulse quickened at the sight as thunder rumbled overhead and lightning lit the darkening sky. Doris wrapped her fingers around the metal and pushed it open. It swung away easily with a screeching creak.

"Come on." She grinned at Ellie as she slipped through the opening.

Ellie, with her hat still squashed onto her head, followed her. They continued up a winding road as more raindrops splattered onto the ground around them.

"Quick!" Doris giggled as she held her hat and broke into a run.

Ellie rushed to follow her before the skies let loose. They

raced around a bend in the overgrown driveway, and the rambling house came into sight.

She slowed, staring at the spooky facade with its glowing windows. Did this house exist in the present-day Salem Falls?

"Hurry!" Doris called as she continued to run ahead.

Another boom of thunder sent Ellie scurrying behind her. She closed the distance between them as they approached the house. They ran up the stone steps to the wide porch. Rain pattered the roof above them as Doris used the snarling lion's head door knocker to announce them.

No one answered. The rain intensified, lightning lit the sky, and thunder rumbled.

Doris glanced at the steady stream of precipitation before she twisted the door knob. She pushed against the door, and it creaked open on its hinges, revealing a dimly lit foyer.

"Mia!" Ellie said before she shook her head. "Sorry, Doris."

"Why do you keep calling me that?"

"You look almost exactly like my best friend in the future. Her name is Mia. It's uncanny, really."

Doris narrowed her eyes. "Interesting."

"Anyway, we shouldn't be letting ourselves into someone's house."

"Alice won't mind. She's probably in the lab." Doris stepped into the dimly lit space. "Alice!"

Ellie ducked inside the door, scanning the gothic space. Thick wood paneling covered the bottom of the walls up to the chair rail. Velvety, burgundy wallpaper rose to the thick, brown crown molding that met the ceiling. She let her eyes rise up the deep brown wooden stairs that disappeared around a corner at the top.

"Alice!" Doris called again. With a huff, she shook her head. "She must be downstairs."

She grabbed Ellie's hand, dragging her forward past a ticking cuckoo clock, toward a door tucked under the stairs.

A glowing green light emanated from underneath it.

"Uhh," Ellie murmured as her eyes went round at the sight, "should we be opening that?"

"I'm sure it'll be fine." Doris tugged open the door. A whirring noise rattled off the walls as the glimmer of green brightened, burning Ellie's eyes.

She squeezed them closed and shielded her face with her hand as Doris pulled her forward. With narrowed eyes, she stumbled down the stairs.

In the basement laboratory, equipment filled the space from wall to wall. Liquids bubbled in a complex network of tubes and beakers. Across the room, a slight figure crouched behind a desk, fingers plugging their ears and goggles covering most of their face.

The humming turned into a high-pitched squeal before something popped. The light began to fade when a beaker exploded, drenching Doris and Ellie with a thick slime.

Ellie's jaw dropped as she wiped away a splotch from her cheek and stared down at it with a disgusted grimace.

"Doris?" The figure leapt from behind the desk, lifting her goggles from her green eyes and plopping them on top of her dark hair.

"Hiya, Alice. We knocked, but no one answered."

"For a reason!" Alice said as she skirted the furniture piece and grabbed a few towels. "This is delicate work."

"Sam?" Ellie said, her brows knitting as she stared at the brunette.

"No, this is Alice. This is the person I told you about. I think she can help us."

"Help you?"

Doris bobbed her head up and down. "Yes. My new

friend, Ellie, is from another time. Twenty twenty-four to be exact. She needs help getting home."

Alice's eyes went wide as she studied Ellie from head to toe. "Why, you're a time traveler?"

Ellie shrugged, still struggling to wipe the sticky goo from her hair. "Apparently."

Alice raced back to the desk and grabbed a pencil and pad before she hurried back to them. She pressed the dull tip against the paper and raised her eyebrows at Ellie.

"How'd you do it?"

"I fell and hit my head. When I woke up, I was a hundred years in the past."

Alice's shoulders slumped, and she clicked her tongue as she scuffed her shoe on the floor. "Oh. I thought you'd have some insight on the technology escaping me in my own time machine."

Ellie side-eyed her. "You have a time machine?"

"Almost. I have a vessel that *will* be a time machine. But... so far, it doesn't work."

Doris stuck her hands on her hips. "Well, we've got to make it work, Alice! Poor Ellie needs to get home."

"Shucks, I wish I could. But the problem is, I don't have much time to spend working on it. I have a job."

"You got a job?" Doris clapped her hands together and grinned.

"Is it selling ice cream at Salem Scoops?"

The two women offered Ellie a confused glance before Doris set her hands on her hips. "Don't tell me you know her, too?"

"She looks exactly like the girl who owns the ice cream shop in my time. Sam is her name."

Alice scribbled on her paper. "This is fascinating. All very fascinating."

"I wish I could say the same, but I'd really just like to get home."

Doris shifted her gaze to the scientist. "How about it, Alice? Can you quit your job and help?"

Alice chewed her lower lip before she shook her head. "I can't. I've been paid in advance. And I promised I'd do the job before All Hallow's Eve."

Doris let her shoulders droop. "Well, aren't you a wet blanket?"

Ellie wrinkled her nose at the term.

"I'm sorry, Doris, but I need the extra dough for my experiments."

"Can't you help us first and solve it later?"

"I can't. I just can't." Alice chewed her lower lip as she slid a disappointed gaze to a large sheet-covered object across the room.

"What's the job? Maybe we can help. If we help you solve it, will you help us?"

"Golly, I'd love to help someone time travel. And I sure could use the help with this investigation."

Doris flung out her hands. "We're in. What is it?"

Alice pressed her lips together and leaned closer. "It's about the corner house on Main Street. I've got to prove it's haunted."

CHAPTER 4

Doris doubled over with laughter, slapping her thighs. "Alice, you slay me!"

Alice wrinkled her nose, clutching the notepad tightly to her chest. "I'm not joking, Doris."

"But ghosts are a bunch of hooey." Doris waved a dismissive hand in the air.

"Well, Flo doesn't think so. She says she can't explain some of the shenanigans that happen in that house. And she's paid me to solve it."

Ellie snorted a laugh. "Well, it can't be haunted."

"Why not?" Alice asked.

"That's...silly. There aren't ghosts. It's got to be something else."

"Says the time traveler," Alice retorted. "Either way, I've got investigating to do."

Doris offered her a curt nod. "Fine. We'll help you solve this mystery as long as you promise to help us get Ellie home."

Alice tapped the pencil against her lips. "All right. But we *have* to concentrate on that. Flo will kill me if I don't have answers soon. She's terrified to stay there."

"She can stay at the boarding house with us until we solve it," Doris said, with a nod.

"You may want to rethink that. She's a bit of a handful, that one."

Doris arched an eyebrow.

"You'll see," Alice said as she crossed the room and tossed the notepad and pencil onto the desk before she unzipped the overalls she wore. She shimmied out of them, revealing a pair of tan houndstooth pants with a matching vest. After rolling down the sleeves of her shimmery beige blouse, she dug through a desk drawer and retrieved a fresh notebook and two pencils.

She hurried across the room to a cabinet and flung it open. "Doris, you carry this."

Ellie knitted her brows as Alice passed the largest camera she'd ever seen to her friend.

"Are we going now?" Doris asked.

Alice nodded. "I'm already late. My experiment cost me some time."

"What were you experimenting on?" Ellie asked as the brunette raced past her toward the stairs.

"I was trying to come up with a spirit catcher. It failed. It's not stable enough yet. Tomorrow's a new day. Tonight, we have to catch a ghost!" Alice darted up the stairs, with Doris and Ellie behind her.

They pushed through the door into the rainy evening.

Alice wrinkled her nose at the precipitation still falling steadily. "My car's around back. We could make a run for it."

They dashed off the porch and hurried around the corner of the porch. An open garage housed a boxy single vehicle inside. Ellie frowned at it as she dodged raindrops, and thunder tumbled overhead again.

They ducked under the cover of the roof. Ellie squeezed into the back seat, shifting around on the uncomfortable bench seat as Alice slid behind the wheel and Doris plopped into the passenger seat.

"I still haven't gotten the hang of driving," Doris said, while Alice started the car. "Chester says women probably lack the ability to tackle something like this."

Ellie slid her eyes closed at the statement.

"That's hogwash. I'm just as good a scientist as my father was. He was so disappointed not to have a son, but I proved them all wrong."

The car barreled down the driveway. Ellie clung to the side as they bounced around on the gravel drive.

"Do women drive in your time, Ellie?" Alice asked.

"Yeah," she huffed out as they swung onto the road.

"All women?" Doris asked.

"Most women, yeah."

"How fascinating," Alice said with a grin, the wheel wobbling underneath her. "And are there women scientists?"

"There are women in everything," Ellie answered. "Women like you broke a lot of glass ceilings, Alice."

The brunette's smile faded, and she crinkled her forehead. "Do you mean beakers?"

"No, ceilings. Glass ceilings is a euphemism for the concept of a social barrier women experienced as they started to work more and more outside of the home."

"Oh," Alice said, "well, I'm happy to be a part of it."

"You mean dames like us working as secretaries?"

"No," Ellie said, with a shake of her head, "I mean dames like us working as executives, doctors, lawyers, business owners. Women are way more than secretaries where I come from."

The buildings of Salem Falls filled in around them as dark clouds continued to hover over the town. "How interesting.

Golly, I hope this investigation goes quickly, so we can talk more about the future."

"While you fix your time machine, right?"

Alice let her lips part for a moment before bobbing her head up and down. "Of course."

Ellie narrowed her eyes at the hesitation but lost the opportunity to question it further when Alice jolted the car to a stop with a quick pump of the brakes as they approached the corner.

A large Victorian faced them with lights glowing inside the windows.

"Come on, ladies," Alice said, grabbing her notebook and pencils. "Let's solve a mystery."

They climbed from the car and hurried up the path to the porch. Alice used the knocker, cowering as another boom of thunder rumbled overhead.

The door swung open on creaky hinges a moment later.

"Val!" Ellie exclaimed.

The woman ran a hand over her curls as she offered Ellie a confused glance. "Who?"

"No, no, this is Florence," Doris corrected, "Flo for short. Sorry, Flo, Ellie's new in town."

"Oh, right. Well, come in, girls." Flo stepped back and motioned them into the small foyer. "I hope you'll be able to give me some answers."

"We will," Alice said, with a nod.

"Right, Ellie's a world-renowned paranormal investigator," Doris said.

"Is that right?" Flo asked. "Well, that'll be something to print."

"Huh?" Ellie questioned as a blonde resembling Hazel wandered from the sitting room.

"World-renowned," she repeated as she jotted something down on her notepad.

Alice drew her chin back to her chest and clicked her tongue as she set a hand on her hip. "What is *she* doing here?"

"Making sure you do your job," Flo said, with a poke of her finger at the scientist. "Whatever you say is going in the papers. I don't want any half-baked ideas or nonsense. I want the truth."

"I was prepared to give it to you. But I don't need Blanche breathing down my neck while I do my investigation."

"Too bad. I don't care what you need. I need answers. And Blanche'll make sure I get them."

Alice set her lips in a thin line as she sighed.

"What did you say your name was again?" Blanche asked Ellie.

"Ellie, Ellie Byrne. Do you work for the Salem Falls Herald?"

Blanche stared at her with round eyes. "That's right. Wow, you must be psychic."

"Or she picked up the paper on her way into town," Flo said, with a grunt.

"Or she's a smart cookie," Doris said, setting her hand on her hip.

Alice waved her hands in the air. "Listen, ladies, we really should get started on the investigation. Can we gather some information from you to start?"

Flo motioned to the sitting room. "Can I offer you some tea?"

"I'll take some," Ellie said as she passed the women, still finding it uncanny how closely she resembled Val.

Flo nodded at them and spun on her heel and disappeared down the hall. Ellie wandered into the sitting room and took a seat on the couch. Doris settled in next to her, with the other two women taking the armchairs.

Alice glared at Blanche, tapping her pencil on her notebook.

Blanche flipped to a fresh page of her own notepad and glanced at Ellie. "Would you mind giving me a quote and some basic information for the article?"

"Uhhh," Ellie stammered, "I'm not that interesting."

"I disagree. If you've been brought in specially for this as a paranormal investigator, you are very interesting."

Ellie considered her talking animals, and now her time travel. "Well, I have some...experience with paranormal things. And I've always loved mysteries."

"Always loved mysteries..."

"And so it was a natural fit for me to help when Sam..." Ellie paused and corrected herself. "Alice asked me."

"And she said she couldn't do it on her own? That she needed help?"

Alice's features scrunched, and she stamped a foot against the floor.

"Oh, no, no," Ellie said, waving a hand in the air. "No, that's not it at all. Alice didn't *ask* for my help. I offered it."

"You...came to town and went to her house to offer help?" Blanche asked, her light eyebrows drawing together under her curly bangs.

"No. I came to town and Mi...uh...Doris mentioned it to me. I was so excited, I asked her to take me to Alice's so I could offer my assistance. She was so gracious to let me tag along."

Flo sashayed in with a tea tray stretched between her hands. She set it on the oval coffee table, using it to shove aside the flowerless vase.

She poured five cups, handing them off before she gathered her own and sat on the loveseat across from Ellie. "Now, what information do you need?"

Alice set her teacup in the saucer and slid it onto the table. "Well, to start, can you share what makes you think the house is haunted?"

Flo sipped her tea, arching an eyebrow as she glanced at them over the rim of her cup. She settled it back in its saucer before she cocked her head, and let her gaze scan them.

"Odd things happen here."

Blanche scribbled it down, while Alice froze. Her shoulders slumped, and she sighed. "I'll need you to be more specific than that."

Flo set her teacup and saucer on the tray with a clatter. "Well, odd noises, gusts of wind from nowhere, doors open when they've been closed, need I go on?"

Both Blanche and Alice scribbled notes.

"Where have these occurred?" Ellie asked. "In one specific room or several?"

"All over the house. I hear things banging when I'm in bed. I investigate, only to find nothing there."

"Where do you hear the banging coming from?" Ellie pressed further.

"It seems to come from everywhere," Flo answered, with wide eyes. "But I can't find it anywhere."

Ellie sipped her tea and nodded. "Right. Okay, when you come down, do you still hear the banging?"

Flo nodded. "I do, but as soon as I start to explore, it stops."

"So, you get to this floor, and the noise ceases," Ellie repeated. "Okay. And then you said gusts of wind from nowhere. Where are you when you feel them?"

Flo blew out a chuckle through her painted red lips and shot a pointed glance at Alice. "Just who is doing this investigation?"

"I'm sorry," Ellie said, "just figured she was writing everything down, so I'd make it easier on her by asking the questions."

"Right," Alice said, poking her eraser at Ellie. "This way, I can really concentrate on the details I need to note."

Flo shot a wry glance at Blanche, who stifled a chuckle before she jotted down something else on her notepad.

"So, where do you feel the wind gusts?"

"When I come down the stairs to investigate, sometimes I'll feel an icy wind rush past me. I think it's the ghost fleeing from whatever naughtiness he's done."

"He?" Ellie inquired. "Have you seen a form?"

"No," Flo answered, "but I've heard him."

"And he's made horrible threats? Said terrible things?" Blanche asked, her eyes wide.

Ellie wrinkled her nose as she shifted her gaze between the two women. "She didn't say that."

"That's right," Doris said, waving a finger in the air, "she didn't say anything like that. Just that she's heard him."

"What did you hear?" Alice asked. "Whispers? Wailing? What?"

"Whispers, mostly. But it's a male voice, not a female. I can't make out the words in most instances."

Ellie narrowed her eyes as she sipped her tea. "Any snippets of words?"

"Quiet. He'll say quiet a lot. That's the only word I can ever hear."

Alice tapped her pencil against her notepad. "No wailing or sounds of distress? Maybe this entity is stuck here and needs help to leave."

Flo shook her head. "No. Sometimes a giggle. No crying or wailing, though."

"Giggle. An evil laugh?" Blanche asked.

Flo gave her a curt nod. "You could say that."

Ellie arched an eyebrow. "Okay, so icy breezes, whispering, and evil laughs. What about the doors? What doors are open?"

"Sometimes it's the front door, sometimes the back.

Sometimes kitchen cupboards are open. Sometimes the basement door is open. It varies."

Alice flipped to a new page and scribbled a few more things before she bit the eraser and studied the page. "Anything else of note?"

"Well, there is the history of the house," Flo said.

Ellie scanned the group as nods met the statement. "What's the history?"

Flo raised her eyebrows and nodded. "It's bloody. Murders, deaths."

"This used to be a stagecoach stop in the early days of the town," Doris said. "Rumor is one of the guests was murdered here. Several people died in the house once it became a private residence."

"And then it was a stop on the underground railroad," Alice added.

"Wow, a lot of history here," Ellie said. "Maybe–"

Her statement was interrupted by a loud bang. Her heart thudded wildly, feeling like it might jump out of her chest. Maybe the place was haunted.

CHAPTER 5

A cold gust of wind swept past Ellie, ruffling the trim of her dress and blowing her hair. She swallowed hard. Maybe they'd get the evidence they needed to prove a ghost haunted this house sooner than she expected.

Her throat went dry as she strained her ears for any sounds of a specter. A giggle split the silence.

Across from her, Flo rolled her eyes. "I assume that's you, Ava."

The brunette rounded the corner with a smile on her red lips. Ellie's eyes went wide as she recognized Scarlett, the news reporter from her own time.

"Yep, sis, it's me."

Flo gave her a disdainful glance. "And who else?"

"Hiya, Flo," a southern voice said before a man appeared at the door and tipped his fedora.

"Rick?" Ellie hissed.

Flo slammed her cup onto the saucer, her face turning purple-red. "How many times have I told you he is not welcome in this house?!"

"As many times as I've told you Tommy is my boyfriend.

And if I can't say goodnight to him inside when it's pouring down rain, then–"

"Then what?" Flo interrupted. "Tell me what you'll do, Ava. Will you move out? I couldn't be so lucky."

Ava's lips twisted into a grimace. "I'm not moving out. This house is mine, too."

"Not according to the deed."

"Mother and Father expressly told you I was supposed to have a home here as long as I wanted it."

"Mother and Father doted on you and spoiled you, simple. I'm not willing to do that. Get him out of this house."

"It's fine, baby, I'll go. I'd hate to rile your sister up any more than she already is." He let his eyes glide over the other women in the living room before he leaned forward and bent the brunette back with a long kiss.

She stumbled, giggling when he set her back on her feet. He tipped his hat to them before he strode from their sight. Ava bit into her lower lip as she twirled a curl around her fingers, watching him go.

"That was an entirely inappropriate display," Flo lectured.

"He loves me. I know it's hard for you to understand, since no man's ever even looked at you twice."

Flo slid her eyes closed and shook her head. "I wouldn't brag about being a mobster's girlfriend. It's not as alluring as you'd like to imagine."

"Oh, it's plenty alluring," Ava answered, with a bat of her eyelashes. "Anyway, I'm going up. Enjoy your…party or whatever it is."

"We'll talk about this later!" Flo shouted as her sister pounded up the stairs and muttered an inaudible response. "I'm so sorry about that. Ava can be…trying."

"That's your sister?" Ellie asked.

"Yes, younger. Obviously. We are nothing alike. Ava likes to put on a show. I prefer to keep to myself."

Ellie smiled politely and nodded at the statement.

After a sip of her tea, Flo settled the teacup into her saucer. "Now, where were we?"

"I think we were just wrapping up your explanation. If you don't mind, we'd like to have a look around the house," Alice said as she slid her pencil into the rings holding her notebook together and flipped it closed.

Flo rose and adjusted her skirt. "When will you have answers?"

"Well," Alice said as she stood, "I'd like to do some research on the stories surrounding the house, and then we may need to set up camp for a night to determine if we experience any of these phenomena."

Flo cocked her head. "If? I *have* experienced them, I assure you."

"Yes, but–"

"But nothing. Alice, I have paid you a sum of money to prove I have a ghost so I may eradicate it. I did not pay you to call me a liar."

"I don't think she said that. But it would be helpful for us to experience what you did, so we can document it," Ellie explained.

"That's right," Alice said. "Now, can you show us all the locations where something strange has happened?"

"Of course." Flo motioned for them to head to the foyer. "We'll start here. This is where I often find the front door standing open after I've crawled from my bed to investigate the banging. And sometimes where I feel the icy gusts of air."

Alice glanced around the space as she nodded.

Ellie wandered to the door and tugged on it. "Latches tightly."

"And locks. I never go to bed without locking it."

"What about your sister, Ava?" Ellie asked.

"I always make certain she is in bed before me. I will have

no…shenanigans under this roof." Flo wagged a finger in the air.

Ellie narrowed her eyes. "She never stays out after you've gone to bed?"

"She has a curfew. She's broken it several times with that…hooligan, but I wait up, then I lock the door after she's gone up."

"Okay," Ellie answered. "Can we see the next space?"

Flo led them down a hall to a large kitchen. "I've often found the cupboard doors open. Sometimes one. Sometimes a few. Or the back door standing open." She motioned to the door tucked in the corner of the space.

Ellie stepped across the tile floor and tugged on the door again. "Any icy breezes here?"

"Yes."

"Do they coincide with when you've found the door open?"

"Not always," Flo answered.

"And which cupboards usually?"

"This one in the corner. And the two by where you're standing." Flo waved a finger at them as Alice made a note. "And then I'll show you the final spot."

They shuffled back into the hall to a door under the staircase. "Here. Sometimes this door is open."

Ellie twisted the knob and tugged it open, staring down the steep stairs. "Have you ever had any encounters down there?"

Flo shook her head. "No."

Ellie arched an eyebrow before flicking her gaze back to the spooky, dark basement. "Really?"

"I never go down there." Flo stared at Ellie, her eyes boring into her. "Ever."

Ellie gulped, shifting her eyes from side to side. "Is there a reason why?"

"Because *that's* probably where the ghost is."

Alice tugged her notebook open again. "What makes you say that?"

"That's where the murder happened. Bad vibes down there." Flo shivered and wrapped her arms around herself. "I want no parts of that basement. I've never been down there in my entire life."

Ellie squinted into the blackness. "Is there anything down there?"

"Maybe a few odds and ends. If we needed any of them, I send Ava. I won't go down there. But we haven't had much use for the few things Mother and Father stored there."

"Do you mind if we take a peek?"

Flo shrugged. "It's your funeral. I'll get you a light."

The woman's heels clicked away as she wandered to the kitchen. She returned moments later with a lantern and matches. After lighting it, she passed it off to Ellie with a half-smirk.

"Good luck."

Ellie crinkled her nose before she raised the lantern above her head and stared into the darkness. "Anyone want to come with me?"

"I'm game," Doris answered, sliding her arm through Ellie's.

"I'll go, too," Alice said.

Ellie nodded and took the first step down onto the creaky tread. She slid her eyes shut as it groaned under her weight. After a steadying breath, she opened them again and took another step. The walls closing them in on both sides opened halfway down the staircase.

Ellie ducked and held out the lantern, trying to spot anything of interest.

A few sheet-draped items filled the dark corners, but most of the basement was empty.

Her heels dug into the gritty floor as she reached the bottom. With the lantern held high, she spun in a slow circle. "I don't see anything."

"Me either," Doris said. "I don't *feel* anything either."

"You mean like a ghost?"

"Yes," the blonde said, with a nod, "like a ghost."

Ellie took a few steps into the heart of the cellar. The light flickered a few times but remained glowing. Alice skirted her, heading for the covered objects.

She lifted up a corner of the sheet. "An old dresser."

"So, just some furniture, like Flo said," Doris answered, with a nod.

Alice set her hands on her hips. "I don't see anything else here."

"Me either. If this place is haunted, it–" Ellie began when the lantern flickered again. She squinted at it, trying to shield the flame from whatever threatened to extinguish it.

An icy breeze swept past her. She froze, casting a glance toward the other two women. "Do you feel that?"

"Feel what?" Doris asked.

"Come here," Ellie whispered.

Alice and Doris joined her in the center of the cellar.

"I don't feel anything," Doris said.

"Just wait. This is the second time the candle has flickered. What's causing it?"

Ellie held her breath, her eyes searching the darkened space for the source of the rogue wind. Seconds later, the flame wobbled again, and cool air caressed her skin.

"There!"

"I feel it!" Doris exclaimed in a hiss, wrapping her arms around her midriff.

Alice cocked her head and stepped forward toward the gust. "Yes, I do, too. Where is it coming from? There is no plausible source for air in a basement."

"Could it be coming from the door upstairs? Maybe it's swirling around in here?" Ellie suggested.

"One way to find out." Alice stalked to the bottom of the stairs and called up them. "Flo, could you shut the door?"

"Shut the door?" Flo responded, her voice incredulous. "Are you sure?"

"We're sure."

The sliver of light streaming down the steps from the floor above slowly turned into a sliver before it disappeared entirely, leaving Alice in the dark.

She hurried back to Ellie's side and waited. Only the sound of their breathing filled the space. Ellie's heart pounded as she waited to confirm her theory…or refute it. She hoped it would not be the latter.

"I think–" Alice began when the flame flickered again. "There it is again. So, it cannot be coming from the upstairs."

"Maybe there's a gap in the door," Doris said.

Alice shook her head. "It's stronger than it's ever been. Science would say it's strongest when it has the least resistance. If the door is closed, that would create resistance."

"It has to be coming from down here, then. But where?" Ellie asked. "There are no windows or doors."

Doris wrung her hands. "Maybe the joint really is haunted."

Alice twisted to face her. "We should go. I'd like to bring equipment back and attempt to monitor for the wayward spirit."

Doris stuck her hands on her hips. "I don't want to sit in this creepy old place if there's a ghost."

"You agreed to help me," Alice chided. "Remember, the longer this takes, the longer your friend is stuck here."

"I'm game to try," Ellie said. "Anything to get back home."

"All right, then," Alice answered, with a nod. "We'll make plans to return tomorrow night."

"Tomorrow night? Can't we come back tonight?" Ellie asked.

"I'd like to make a few tweaks to my equipment first. We'll plan for tomorrow and hope to experience the phenomenon again."

Ellie heaved a sigh and shook her head. "All right, fine."

They abandoned their basement search, climbing the stairs and pushing through the door into the hall.

"Well?" Flo asked, her hand pressed against her chest and face devoid of color.

"I think you may have something here, Florence. We plan to return tomorrow with a whole host of equipment to capture the presence."

Blanche gasped. "Do you mean…you'll bottle the ghost?"

"Certainly not. We must first test to determine *if* a ghost exists," Alice said. "And then, if it does, we'll determine what to do with it."

"You'll keep me updated?" Blanche asked. "I'm busy tomorrow night."

"Yes, of course," Flo said.

Alice rolled her eyes at the woman. "Fine. Until tomorrow, then."

They said their goodnights before they exited the house and climbed back into the car. Alice dropped them off at the boarding house. With plans made for her to pick them up tomorrow, she drove off into the darkness.

Ellie slogged up the stairs to what would become her B&B and pushed through the door. "Whew, what a night."

Doris chewed her fingernail as Mopsie barreled down the stairs and wagged her tail at them. "I agree. I wonder if we'll catch the darned thing."

"Did you bring us anything?" Kitty asked from her perch on the stairs.

"Doesn't look like it," Mopsie answered.

"Dumb Doras." Kitty shook a paw at them before disappearing up the stairs.

"Well, I guess I'll head to bed," Ellie said, with a sigh.

"Just a moment, you must be starving, in addition to tired. Could you stand to help me make a sandwich?"

Ellie smiled at the woman and nodded. "That would be great. Mind if I change first?"

"Not at all. I think I'll do the same. We'll just be two gals having our late dinner in our pajamas." Doris lifted a shoulder as she grinned at Ellie and led her up the stairs.

Ellie headed for her regular bedroom before she remembered the house wasn't hers in this time. She veered off and wandered down to the last door in the hall.

As she shoved the door closed behind her, she spun to find the two pets waiting on her bed. Mopsie rose to all fours, wagging her tail.

"Stop it, Mopsie, you're shaking me apart," Kitty exclaimed.

Ellie approached the bed and rubbed the dog's head. She stopped her wiggling and lowered her rear end to the mattress.

"Listen, Elsie," Kitty said.

"Ellie," Ellie corrected. "It's Ellie."

"Oh, oops. Sorry." The sarcasm dripped from the cat's pearly white fangs as she offered an awkward smile.

"You did that purpose."

"Why would I have done that? Maybe because you didn't bring me anything to eat. Or maybe because you called me Cleo earlier. My name is *Kitty*."

"I'm sorry. I was confused. I'm not from here. Don't you remember?"

"Riiiight, you're from the future." Her green eyes went round as she stared at Ellie.

"I am. I can't help it."

"Sure you are."

"I believe you, Ellie," Mopsie said, her forehead wrinkled.

Ellie traced the folds as she rubbed her head. "Thanks, Mopsie. I appreciate that. It's nice to know *someone* believes me." She shot a pointed glance at the cat before kicking off her shoes.

"Listen, Ellie, we need to talk."

"Okay."

"You have to help us," the cat said.

Ellie shimmied out of her dress before tugging off her stockings. "With?"

"Doris. She's dumb."

"She seems okay to me." Ellie plopped on the bed and pulled on her pajama pants.

"She never answers us. Well, sometimes she does, but sometimes I'll ask her a question, and she acts like she can't hear me."

Ellie slid her arms into her shirt and pulled it closed to button. "I don't think she can hear you."

"But you can," Mopsie said.

"Yeah, I can. I can hear the animals in the future, too. In fact, you two look just like my own pets."

"Cleo?" Kitty asked.

"Yes. Cleo is my black cat."

"What's my name in the future, Ellie?" Mopsie asked.

"Stupid," Kitty answered. "You're not in the future. It's another dog."

"Lola. Her name is Lola." Ellie pulled her robe around her shoulders and sighed. "And I really miss her. And Cleo. I want to go home."

"Maybe you have to do something before you can," Mopsie said.

"Like help us," Kitty added. "Help Doris talk to us."

Ellie wrinkled her nose as she shoved her feet into her slippers. "I thought it was to solve the haunted house thing."

"Not that," Kitty assured her.

"Right," Ellie said as she rose. "Because I'm certain you know for sure what I need to do to get home."

"I'm glad you recognize my authority on this subject. Now, when will you begin the plan to talk to Doris?"

"We'll see." Ellie shuffled to the door and tugged it open.

She navigated downstairs to the kitchen. Doris appeared a few minutes later, her blonde hair up in pincers, with a scarf wrapped around it. They made their sandwiches and settled at the table.

"So," Doris said as she licked a glob of mayonnaise off her thumb, "do you think there's a ghost in that house?"

Ellie bit into the ham sandwich and chewed as she considered it. "Well, I'm not sure it's a ghost. But maybe we'll get more information tomorrow night."

"I'm not sure I want to," Doris said.

Ellie let her gaze fall to the table, studying the grain. "I really hope we do. I really want to go home."

"Aww, I'm sorry," Doris said, her features twisting with concern. "I didn't mean–"

"I know," Ellie said, sliding her hand across the table to squeeze Doris's. "I just don't want to be stuck back here. And I'm afraid I may be."

CHAPTER 6

Tears formed in Ellie's eyes as she chewed her lower lip, willing them to recede.

Doris patted her hand. "Aw, Doll, don't fret. I'm certain Alice will find a way to help. She's wonderful with science things like this."

Ellie sniffled and nodded, offering her a weak smile. "Right. I'm just tired. And panicking."

"Tell her about us. I bet you'll go right home if you do that," Kitty said, rubbing against Ellie's legs.

"Aw, look, Kitty knows you're upset and is trying to comfort you. Kitty, you're so kind."

"I am not. I want her to do something for us." The cat shook her paw as she glared at Doris.

Ellie reached down and stroked her head.

Mopsie approached and gave her fingers a lick. "I'm being kind."

Doris cocked her head as she studied the animals with Ellie. "You know, sometimes I think animals know what we're saying and can understand when we need a little extra love."

"Now's the perfect time to tell her about us," Kitty encouraged.

Ellie bit her lower lip and flicked her gaze at Doris as she took a bite of her sandwich. Maybe the cat had a point. Maybe it would work. She'd inexplicably traveled back in time. In the realm of all things possible, maybe telling Doris her dog and cat could speak would correct the universe.

Ellie licked her lower lips before she plowed into the conversation. "You know, Doris, I think you're onto something there."

"How so?"

"Well, what if…the animals could understand us and answer. But not all of us could hear them?"

Doris chewed a bite of her food as she considered it. "I'm not sure I understand. Are you saying I've got talking pets?"

Ellie smiled and flicked up her eyebrows. "Maybe."

Doris set her sandwich down on her plate and eyed the two animals across the room. "Kitty, can you speak?"

"Of course I can. I've been talking to you for five years."

Doris tilted her head, shifting her gaze to the dog. "And what about you Mopsie?"

"Sure," the dog said, leaping to her feet and wagging her tail.

Doris smiled at them both. "Wouldn't it be a more interesting world if they could?"

"But…" Ellie began before sucking in a breath. "You bet it would."

"What a fun idea. Maybe I'll mention it to Alice. I'd wager she'd have a ball testing it out and seeing if we can communicate with them."

Ellie plastered a smile onto her face before she returned to her meal.

"Dumb Doras," Kitty grumbled before she stalked from the room.

They polished off their sandwiches and called it a night. Ellie shuffled past her room with a forlorn glance before continuing to the one she was currently staying in.

She climbed into bed and tugged up the covers as she prepared for a sleepless night. She squeezed her eyes closed, trying to stop herself from crying when a creak made her pop them open again.

Her heart thudded, and she scanned the room. The door stood open, though she'd closed it when she came in. How had it–

A black shadow leapt in the air, landing at her feet.

Ellie blew out a sigh of relief. "Kitty."

"And Mopsie," the dog said as she clicked her way across the floor and jumped up next to Ellie.

"Shouldn't you both be sleeping with Doris?"

"She's a bed hog," Kitty answered. "She throws her arms everywhere. Plus, she can't talk to us like you can."

Ellie sighed as she sank back into the pillow. "Maybe Alice can fix that."

"Do people talk to animals all the time in the future?" Kitty asked.

"No. Just me. I talk to Lola and Cleo. And Roxy, one of the raccoons."

"Well, then Alice didn't fix it, did she?"

Ellie drummed the mattress on either side of her. "I guess not."

"What's wrong, Ellie?" Mopsie asked.

"Oh, I'm just wondering if I'll ever get home."

Mopsie nudged her hand with her cold, wet nose. "If you don't, you can stay here with us. We like you."

Ellie rubbed the dog's head. "I appreciate that. But I really want to go home. And telling Doris you could talk didn't help."

"Maybe if you solve the mystery at the haunted house," Mopsie said.

Ellie stared at the ceiling as moonlight painted it. "Maybe."

Kitty licked her paw. "Everyone knows the story about that."

"What is it?"

"It's haunted. Some swell got bumped off by another guest. And now he haunts the joint."

"I guess we'll find out when we stay there tomorrow night."

"Stay there tomorrow night?" Kitty exclaimed. "You can't stay there tomorrow night. The ghost will get you."

"That's what we're hoping."

"You want a ghost to get you?" Mopsie asked.

"No, I want to find the ghost so Alice can help me go home."

"You should take us with you. We have way better senses than you do," Kitty said.

Ellie lifted her head and stared down at the cat's glowing eyes. "That's not a half-bad idea. Maybe we should."

"I want to go," Mopsie said. "I like to go. I will bark at all the ghosts."

"I'll bet you will. If you're anything like Lola, we won't have a moment's peace."

"I'll catch that old ghosty. He won't know what hit him when I sniff him out. We'll have this solved in no time," Kitty promised.

Ellie offered them both a smile and pat on the head before she settled into the covers. With a plan in place, she drifted off to sleep, with the hopes of returning to her own time soon.

Bright sunshine shone through the windows the next

morning, though the trees outside Ellie's window still dripped with the rain from the storms the night before.

Ellie crawled from her bed with bleary eyes and stretched before she tugged her robe around her and stuffed her feet into her slippers. She wandered down the stairs, her spirits lifting as she smelled bacon frying.

"Hi, Doll, how'd you sleep?" Doris asked as she twisted to face her. Mopsie rose from her spot at Doris's feet and wagged her tail while Kitty opened her mouth in a wide yawn.

"Oh, pretty well, considering I just time-traveled a century to the past," Ellie said as she crossed to the stove. "Can I help with anything?"

"You can make the toast and butter it," Doris said as she pushed the crackling bacon around in the pan.

Ellie shuffled away, stopping dead. "Where's the toaster?"

"On the table, of course," Doris said, poking the pronged fork toward it.

Ellie crossed to it and frowned. "What do I do with it?"

Doris set her fork down and wiped her hands on her apron as she crossed to it. "Haven't you ever seen an electric toaster?"

"I've seen them, but they're way different than this."

Doris loaded a slice of bread and started it toasting. "Now, just watch it, then turn it so the other side toasts."

"Turn it!?" Ellie cried, her voice incredulous.

"Yes. Unless you like just one side toasted."

"How inconvenient. In the future, it toasts both sides at once."

"No kidding! How swanky. You must live in the lap of luxury."

Ellie set her chin on a fist as she stared at the bread. "Hardly, but I can't complain. I've had some lucky breaks in my life."

"Including falling backward in time, right?" Doris asked, giving her a wink.

Ellie turned the bread around to toast the other side. "I'm not sure if this is lucky, but at least I found someone willing to help. You're so much like my friend Mia, it's amazing."

Doris removed the bacon slices and put them on a plate before she cracked eggs and fried them in the grease. Ellie busied herself buttering the toast. In minutes, she had a full meal in front of her with a cup of tea.

"What's it like in the future, Ellie?" Doris asked after biting into her bacon.

Ellie shrugged, cutting off a piece of the crispy egg white. "Everything is much more convenient."

"I can't imagine a world with women doing things men do and not being questioned or criticized."

"Oh, we still get criticized plenty, but there aren't the restrictions you gals have in this time."

"Fascinating. I just may try Alice's time machine with you and find out for myself."

"I think you'd like it. Though, I'm not sure how Mia would react to a lookalike."

"We could play long-lost twins."

A knock interrupted their conversation. Mopsie flew from the room with a screech. Doris dabbed her lips with her napkin as she rose.

"Stop that, Mopsie!" Doris shouted as she hurried down the hall to the front door.

Ellie sipped her tea as footsteps approached.

"Look who I found," Doris said as Alice strode into the room behind her. "Tea, Alice?"

"Yes, please." Alice slid into a chair and set her notebook on the table. "Good morning, Ellie."

"Good morning. All ready to go ghost-hunting?"

"Yes. Though it appears you aren't." Alice eyed Ellie's robe.

"Oh, no, I haven't gotten dressed yet."

"But you came to breakfast."

Ellie stopped mid-chew, parsing the statement. She swallowed the bite of toast. "Yeah. Is that a problem?"

Doris waved it away as she delivered the teacup to Alice.

After blowing on it, the woman sipped her tea. "Do people in the future eat in their night things?"

"I often eat in my jammies, yes. Breakfast, dinner, whatever."

"Interesting. The future seems to be a free-for-all."

Ellie wiggled her eyebrows. "Well, I guess it's a lot more relaxed than here. People wear pajama pants to shop. Although to be fair, you can shop from your home now."

"Oh, is this using a catalog? I've heard talk about this fad," Doris said.

"No, we have something called the Internet. It connects people all over the world and allows you to buy things."

"How do you get them?" Alice asked.

"Someone brings them to you."

"How do you pay for them?" Doris questioned.

"With a credit card. You can charge it, and then pay it later."

"Amazing," Alice hissed before a sip of her tea. "Well, I hope to visit you there one day. But first, we must focus on this investigation."

"Do you really think there's a paranormal disturbance?" Ellie asked.

"I hope to find one. I'd be famous if I could prove life after death." The corners of Alice's lips turned up as she stared into space.

Ellie wiggled her eyebrows as she slid her eyes sideways

toward the two animals in the room. "Or if you could prove something else. Anyway, I should get dressed."

"Yes, please do. I had hoped to collect you both before I went into town to pick up a few things. Then, we'll regroup at the mansion, modify my ghost-hunting tools and head over to collect data."

Ellie finished the last of her tea, dabbed the corners of her lips with her napkin, and rose. "I won't be long."

She hurried up the stairs to change into the second dress Doris had given her. One attempt at getting home had failed. She'd broached the subject of talking pets with Doris, and she hadn't magically swirled back to the future. Maybe if they could solve the case of the haunted house, she'd return then.

As she shimmied into the pink shin-length sheath, she pondered the mystery. It couldn't be ghosts, could it? Even after time traveling, she couldn't believe that.

But what else was it? There was indeed an unexplainable breeze. There had to be a reason.

She slipped on her shoes and headed downstairs to join the others.

"All ready?" Doris asked.

Ellie nodded. "Yep. Oh, uh, I wonder if we should take Kitty and Mopsie."

Doris cocked her head. "Whatever for?"

"They have keener senses than we do. They may be able to alert us to something we miss."

"An excellent idea, Ellie," Alice said, waving a finger in the air, "yes. Let's pick them up on our way back to the house later."

"Fine by me," Doris answered as she grabbed her purse.

In Alice's car, they trundled into town, made a few purchases at the hardware store, then headed back to the mansion. With warm cups of tea on the cool autumn day, the trio worked to modify a microphone to record sound.

Ellie studied the large mic in front of her as Alice fiddled with another piece of equipment. She depressed three buttons on the tape deck. The two wheels began to whirl around.

"All right, Ellie, give it a go."

Ellie leaned forward toward it. "Test, test, test."

Alice nodded and clicked off the tape, rewound it, then played it back. Ellie's voice sounded clearly through it.

"We've done it!" Doris cried.

"Yes, now if only I could get this real-time image capturer working, we'd really be in business."

"Real-time image capturer?" Ellie asked.

Alice nodded. "Yes. I'd like to take this camera and make it so it captures a series of images like a moving picture."

Ellie stared at the large item, a chuckle nearly escaping her lips.

"Have they done that in your era?" Doris asked.

"And then some. I have a device about this big," Ellie answered, using her hands to display the size of a smartphone, "that will do all of this and more."

"Interesting. What do you call a device like that?"

"A smartphone," Ellie answered.

"A smartphone," Alice repeated. "How fascinating. Well, no time to discuss the particulars now. We should pack up the gear, grab the four leggeds, and head over to the house. I'd like to solve this mystery tonight."

They spent the next hour stowing all the equipment in the car before climbing inside and driving the short distance to the boarding house. With Mopsie on her lap and Kitty with Doris, they rode to the Victorian.

"I'm so excited," Mopsie said as the car rolled to a stop.

"Yeah, we're going to sniff out a ghost," Kitty called from the front seat.

"Okay, Kitty, let's go see if we can solve this mystery," Doris said as she climbed from the car.

They shuttled the pets inside and, after a brief squabble with Flo about their presence, settled them in the living room before carting in all the gear.

Thunder rumbled overhead as they dragged in the last of the equipment and carried it down to the basement. With help from Ellie and Doris, Alice set up her monitoring system, and they settled in to wait for any action.

Mopsie sat at attention, expecting to hear or see something. After an hour, she slouched down and laid her head on her paws with a deep sigh.

"I guess the dog hasn't picked up on anything," Alice said with as big an exhale as Mopsie's.

"Doesn't appear to have." Doris motioned to the black cat stretched out on the floor next to her. "Kitty either."

Alice tapped her pencil against her lips. "Perhaps pets aren't as sensitive to the supernatural as we first thought."

"Maybe–" Ellie began when both Kitty and Mopsie snapped up their heads.

Mopsie's lips formed an O as she sucked in a breath, preparing to bark.

Ellie put a hand on her head. "Shh."

"I hear something," the dog answered.

"They've detected something," Alice whispered. "Both of them."

"But what?" Doris glanced around in search of whatever had brought them both to attention.

Ellie leaned closer to the dog. "What do you hear?"

"Bang, bang, bang, thud, thud, thud," Mopsie answered.

Ellie strained her ears to listen for noise. A second later, a muffled thump sounded overhead.

"There!" she hissed, poking a finger toward the ceiling. "I heard it."

"Me, too," Doris said as Kitty leapt to her feet.

"Me, three," the cat added.

"And me," Alice said, her eyes scanning the ceiling. "Someone or some*thing* is up there."

CHAPTER 7

Ellie swallowed hard as another *thud* banged above them. With both of the house's occupants in bed for the night, no one else could be roaming the floor above.

"Sh-should we go up and check it out?" Ellie asked, suddenly feeling less brave about a ghost encounter than she had earlier.

Alice nodded and picked up a large flashlight. "We have to. This could be the break we're looking for!"

Ellie nodded, squashing her fear as she climbed to her feet. What's the worst a ghost could do to her? She took a wobbly step toward the staircase. Maybe she didn't want to find out.

Alice passed her, her light beam swinging as she went. "Come on, ladies, before we miss it!"

The dog and cat climbed to their feet, too, and followed behind them. As they reached the top of the stairs, Mopsie barreled past them and raced toward the back door with a yip.

They hurried behind the dog to the kitchen.

The canine stood at the back door, wagging her tail. "Someone's out there."

"I smell someone, too." Kitty sneezed twice. "Wearing a ton of perfume."

Ellie squinted out the window into the darkness. A streak of red raced past. "Someone's running through the yard!"

Alice raced to the door and flung it open, pushing through the screen door. "Hurry, they're getting away!"

The light swept past the window as Alice chased after the fleeing individual. Doris flew out the door after the scientist.

"Stay here," Ellie told the animals as she followed behind the other two women.

Her feet pounded across the grass as she hastened to reach the sidewalk.

"This way!" Alice called from ahead of her, waving her light down the street.

Ellie panted as she continued forward, following Alice and Doris as they hung a left and continued through the town. A moment later, the diner came into view. Now called "Al's," its darkened windows indicated it was not currently open.

Doris stood in the parking lot, spinning as she scanned the space. "Where did she go?"

"Where's Alice?" Ellie huffed out as she reached the woman.

"Around back, I think."

A second later, the light bobbled around the corner of the building. "Where is she?"

"I don't know. Maybe she went into the woods."

"No," Alice said. "She went inside, and she couldn't have gotten out the back door fast enough to disappear in the woods without me catching her."

"She? Inside?" Ellie questioned, flicking her gaze to the empty building. "Doesn't look like anyone is there."

Alice stamped a foot on the ground. "Yes, she was wearing a red dress. She went right through the front door. I know because the moonlight glinted off it as it closed, and I could just make out a shadow inside. She went toward the back, and I raced around the side of the building but found no one."

Doris scanned the windows. "Should we look? Maybe she's hiding in there."

"Let's try. We'll know if the front door is open." Alice strode toward the diner.

They climbed the few stairs and pressed inside. Alice swept her flashlight around, while Doris ducked to check under the tables.

"Nothing," she said with a shrug as she rose.

"I'll check the kitchen, you ladies check the facilities." Alice left them in the moonlit diner as she skirted the counter and headed to the back.

Ellie pulled open the door to the men's room, while Doris checked the ladies', but neither found anyone inside.

"Anything?" Alice asked as she returned.

"Nope, you?" Ellie asked.

"Nothing. But she must be here."

Doris set her hands on her hips. "Are you sure she didn't give you the slip out the back door?"

"I'm certain. I would have seen her."

"Well, she's not here." Doris threw her arms out to the sides. "So, you must have missed her."

"But I didn't!"

"Shh." Ellie waved a hand in the air before pressing a finger to her lips.

"Sorry, Ellie, I didn't mean to argue, but–"

Ellie shushed her again, holding a hand up in the air. "Listen."

The ladies strained their hearing.

"Do you hear that? Sounds like…a drum or a beat."

They stood silent in the darkened diner again before Alice began to nod her head. "Yes, yes, I hear it, too."

"Where is it coming from? Outside?" Doris asked.

"We didn't hear it when we were out there."

Ellie crossed to the door and pushed it open. "No noise out here. Just in here."

Alice's flashlight fell to the floor. "It sounds as though it's coming from below us."

"But there's nothing under the diner," Doris said.

"Or is there?" Alice trained her light on the floor tiles and cocked her head. "It would explain where our red-dress lady disappeared to."

"What would be below the diner? A bunker of some kind?"

"And how is it accessed?" Alice asked, swinging her flashlight around the space again. "Come on, ladies, let's look around again."

They spread out and searched until Alice shouted from near the restrooms. "Over here. The music is louder from inside this coat closet."

Alice trained her light beam on the wood paneling at the back. Ellie squinted at it, noting something odd. She grabbed the light and raised it, using her finger to trace the outside of a square panel at forehead height.

"What is that?" Alice asked.

"I'm not sure. I wonder if we can move it."

Ellie pressed on it and tried to slide it to the side. It gave way, and light poured from the small opening. A pair of eyes appeared through it a second later.

"What's the password?"

Ellie's jaw dropped. "Jake?"

"That's right."

The panel slid closed again and the entire back wall fell

away as a man who looked like Jake Braeden's twin pulled it open and motioned for them to enter. Jazz music filled the air as they stepped through the opening.

Ellie wrinkled her nose at the man, but before she could say anything, Doris and Alice tugged her further inside.

"I can't believe this!" Doris squealed.

"Me neither. This must be a speakeasy."

"Run by the mob!" Doris said.

"What?" Ellie asked as they made their way into the secret bar.

Flappers danced in their glad rags to the peppy jazz music and fedora-covered heads nodded together at tables as clouds of smoke floated over them.

"The mob. The kid at the door. That's Bugsy Malone. Right-hand man to none other than Tommy Two Toes, Salem Falls' own mob boss. We met him last night at Flo's."

Alice nodded. "Yes, it makes sense. The red-dress woman must have come in here. And I bet I know who she is."

"Tommy Two Toes," Ellie murmured as Alice rose to her tiptoes to scan the crowd. "Val's grandfather?"

"Somebody say my name, ladies?" a southern accent asked.

They swung around to find the man resembling Rick in the future standing behind them.

"You!" Alice said, poking a finger at him. "This is your secret and illegal club, isn't it?"

Tommy held up his hands in defeat. "I admit to nothing." He grinned at them.

"You louse!" Alice said.

"Hey now, this is just a couple of friends listening to music, having a good time."

Ellie raised an eyebrow at him as she glanced around him at the bar. "Isn't alcohol illegal?"

"Who says I'm serving giggle water?"

"The amount of giggling in here," Ellie countered before she stormed to the bar. "I'll have what they're having."

The bartender shot Tommy a glance before he slid his gaze back to Ellie. "Ginger ale?"

"That's *not* ginger ale. It's hooch."

"Hey now, let's not hurl accusations. You won't like me when I'm angry."

Bugsy approached, straightening his jacket. "There a problem here, Boss?"

"Yeah, this doll seems to think we're doing something illegal here. She doesn't understand that we're all just having a good time."

"I don't care what you're doing here, to be quite honest," Ellie said, setting a hand on her hip. "What I do care about is that it's you who have been 'haunting' the house."

Tommy chuckled as Ava sidled up to him, and he slipped his arm around her waist.

Ava waved and giggled as Tommy kissed her on the cheek. "Hi girls, so glad you could join us."

"So, you are here." Alice put her hands on her hips. "I thought as much. You're the ghost, not him."

Ava flicked her dark hair over her red-clad shoulder. "I don't know what you're talking about."

"It's you causing the ruckus. You and your sneaking out."

"Of course not. Flo would never even hear me climbing across the roof on that side of the house. It's not me."

Ellie shook her head. "No, it's not her." She flicked her gaze to Tommy and Bugsy. "It's them."

"What do you mean?" Doris asked.

"I mean there's no ghost in that house. There are just two mobsters making hooch in the basement."

Alice shook her head. "There's no apparatus for that."

"Come on," Ellie said, with a huff, "I'll show you."

Tommy grabbed her elbow. "Now, just a second, Doll–"

Ellie wrangled her arm from his grasp. “I don’t want to get you in trouble with the law. I just want to solve a mystery and go home.”

Ava stepped in front of her. “Flo will turn them in. You can’t!”

Doris stepped forward, her hands on her hips. “So, it’s true?”

Ava’s lower lip jutted out. “Yes. No one uses that stupid basement. And Flo won’t even go in it. It’s the perfect place to make a little moonshine for Tommy’s business venture.”

“Business venture?” Alice asked. “This isn’t a business venture, it’s criminal activity.”

“I wouldn’t talk, sister,” Tommy said. “Who knows what goes on up at that creepy old house you have.”

“Nothing illegal.”

“Prove it,” Bugsy said. “A dame like you shouldn’t be messing around with all that stuff.”

“And how do we know you’re not making your own hooch?” Tommy asked.

“I most certainly am not!”

“Wait, wait,” Doris said, with a shake of her head. “How are you making giggle water in the basement when there’s nothing there to make it with?”

Ava heaved a sigh. “There’s another room, hidden behind a piece of furniture. We slip inside in the middle of the night, make the giggle water, bottle it up, and bring it here.”

“So, the whispering…” Alice began.

“Is us talking.”

“The open doors and cupboards?” Doris questioned.

“Guilty,” Ava said. “Sometimes we leave things open because we’re in a hurry.”

“And the breezes,” Ellie said, “are coming from the other room.”

“But how? And why couldn’t we smell the alcohol?”

"There's a small window we use to vent. That's where the air comes from."

"Well, that solves that," Alice said, with her shoulder slumped. "I guess there isn't a ghost after all."

"How are we going to explain this to Flo?"

"You can't tell her. She'll turn us in!" Ava said.

"Maybe she ought to! You shouldn't be sneaking around in her house, making hooch!" Alice said.

Tommy stiffened, pounding one fist into his other palm. "Looks like we've got a problem here."

"Wait just a second," Ellie interrupted, getting between Tommy and Alice. "There's no reason for there to be a problem."

"Far as I can see, there is one."

"There isn't. You have to stop making alcohol in Flo's basement."

"Why? We'll just tell her it's the ghost? Alice, can't you just tell her the house *is* haunted?"

"But Alice doesn't have any proof of that. Plus, what if she starts calling in psychics to cleanse the house and someone else stumbles upon your little operation?"

Ava pouted, shooting a glance at Tommy. "Sorry, baby, looks like I messed up big-time."

Ellie shook her head. "Not necessarily. Stop making the hooch at the house. Make it somewhere else."

"Where?" Bugsy asked. "We need privacy and space."

"Alice's."

Alice's eyes went wide. "What? No!"

"It's private, and you can do it in exchange for a generous rental fee that will help fund your scientific experiments."

"Ellie!" Alice hissed, stamping a foot on the floor.

Ellie held a finger up in the air and spun to face Alice. "Stop being a stick in the mud. Prohibition ends in less than a decade. It's fine."

Alice pressed her lips together as she considered it. She shifted her gaze to Doris. "What do you think?"

Doris lifted a shoulder. "I don't mind a bit of giggle water sometimes."

"Neither do I. In truth, I still have some of my father's whiskey, and I take a nip every so often."

"It's not that much of a crime. So much so that they repeal this in a few years."

Alice flicked her gaze between Ellie and Doris before she nodded and pushed between them. "All right. But we must discuss the terms of the rental fee. And I want a small portion of the batch. And entry for Doris and I into the club any time."

Tommy puckered his lips. "Fine. We'll move our equipment over after we've come to terms."

"We'll meet tomorrow morning. Until then, I have to deliver the bad news to Flo that it's just a loose latch causing her issue."

Ava bit her lower lip. "Do you think she'll buy it?"

"If she doesn't, I'll simply tell her Tommy has been making romantic overtures by calling to you from the ground and that's the whispering she's heard."

"She'll buy that," Ava said, with a nod.

"Looks like we're done here." Ellie stepped toward the door.

Ava grabbed her arm. "Ellie. Thanks."

Ellie gave her a nod before Alice and Tommy set a time to talk terms. The ladies left the speakeasy behind and wandered back to the corner Victorian to pack up the pets, equipment, and deliver the news.

A surprised Flo clutched at her robe as Alice explained that she'd found the back door unlatched, creating a breeze that blew open a few of the doors, including the loose cupboard closures in the kitchen.

She'd argued about the cause, but after cleverly loosening the screws earlier, Alice demonstrated the door's failure to properly catch.

Flo shook her head as Alice tightened the screws so the door would properly latch. "Golly, I hope Blanche doesn't print any of this. I'll call her right away and make sure it doesn't appear in the papers. I feel so foolish."

"I'm sure she'll oblige," Alice answered.

They drove back to the boarding house as the sun rose higher in the sky. Ellie slogged through the door with Doris, Mopsie, and Kitty.

"What a night!" Doris said. "How about a hearty breakfast before we try for a nap?"

"Nah, I'm not hungry," Ellie answered, with a frown.

"Why the long face, Doll?"

Ellie threw her hands out to the sides. "I'm still here. I thought if I solved the mystery, I'd go home. But I'm still here."

"You're stuck," Kitty said.

"It's okay, Ellie," Mopsie added, "we like you."

Ellie patted the dog's head as tears formed in her eyes.

"Oh, Doll, I'm sorry." Doris patted Ellie's arm as she shook her head. "Say, how about if I give Alice a ring, and we'll brainstorm a way to send you back?"

Ellie pressed her lips together in a weak smile. "Thanks, but–"

"You can't refuse. You helped us! Now it's our turn." Doris stalked to the phone in the foyer and picked it up, giving the operator the information she needed to reach the mansion. A moment later, she spoke again. "Say, Alice, are you too tired to help Ellie figure out how to get home? She's awfully upset about it."

Ellie chewed her lower lip as she stroked the dog's thick fur.

"Well, that's wonderful. We'll be right up!" Doris set the receiver down and spun to Ellie with a grin. "Alice says to come right up. She has an idea, and she thinks it'll send you right home!"

CHAPTER 8

Nervous energy filled Ellie as she walked up the road next to Doris. Thunder rumbled overhead again as another storm rolled into town. The wind picked up, sending her hair flying.

A bark sounded behind them as they walked.

"That sounded like Mopsie," Doris said as she stopped and glanced behind her.

Her jaw dropped as the miniature bulldog barreled toward them. Behind her, a small black cat stalked up the road.

Doris set her hands on her hips. "Mopsie! Kitty! What are you two doing here? How did you get out?"

Mopsie raced to Ellie. "We couldn't let you go without saying goodbye."

Ellie bent to pet the dog. Would this be goodbye? As much as she hoped so, it would be hard to leave her newfound friends. "Aw, I'll miss you, too, Mopsie."

Kitty sauntered up behind the dog. "I just wanted a field trip."

Ellie chuckled, her tears receding a bit at the cat's words.

She tousled the feline's fur. Kitty leaned away from her and flicked her paw in the air.

"Poor babies. They're going to miss you if this works."

"And I'll miss them," Ellie said as she rose. "And you. And Alice. But boy, will I be glad to be home."

Doris smiled at her and turned back toward the mansion. "Then let's go and get you home."

They completed their route to the mansion, pushing inside rather than knocking.

"I'm downstairs, ladies!" Alice called from the basement.

They descended to the lab below, with the animals in tow.

"What's this?" Alice asked as she set her hands on her hips.

"Sorry, apparently, Mopsie and Kitty couldn't bear not to see Ellie off. You know, she had an interesting idea last night. She said maybe pets can communicate with us. I wonder if we could work on that together as your next project."

"Well, considering that I can scrap my ghost trap, it may be a good direction to go in," Alice said, with a nod. "I'll need something to occupy my time."

Ellie patted her thighs as the conversation progressed. "I hate to break up the party, but I'm dying to know your idea to send me home."

Alice waved a finger in the air and stalked across the cavernous space toward a massive object hidden by a sheet. With the arch of one eyebrow, she whipped off the sheet.

Ellie stepped closer, scrunching her features as she stared at the large ball. It looked like a diver's helmet, only large enough to fit the entire diver inside. "What is it?"

"A time machine. I mentioned it when we first met."

Ellie circled the metal contraption. "How does it work?"

"Well, that's the thing. It doesn't. Yet."

Ellie twisted back to glance at the woman. "Yet?"

"Mm-hmm. I mean, theoretically, it's flawless."

"But it doesn't work. How will this help me?"

"It's not that it doesn't work…I've never had it running."

"Why?" Ellie asked.

"I've never harnessed enough power to get it going properly. But I think if I can do that, it would work and send you back to where you came from. All we'll need to do is program in the date, power it up, and let it do its work."

Doris raised her shoulders to her ear. "How can we power it?"

Alice pressed her lips together. "Well, I need about one-point-two-one gigawatts of power."

"Giga-whats?" Doris asked.

Ellie scoffed at the figure. "That seems like a lot. How can we generate that?"

"We can't," Alice answered.

"Then it's hopeless," Doris cried.

"No," Alice responded. "It's not hopeless. *We* can't generate that kind of power, but Mother Nature can. And she's about to do it very soon."

Thunder rumbled overhead, and all gazes went to the ceiling.

Ellie shot a wide-eyed glance at Alice. "No."

"Am I missing something?" Doris asked.

"She's going to harness a lightning bolt to power this thing."

Alice stalked across the room and grabbed a heavy cord. "I think if I climb onto the roof and set up a lightning rod, we'll get a nice strike that'll start this thing up. All we need to do is get you inside, set it, and wait."

Ellie stared back at the metal ball, her features scrunching. "Uhh…"

"You think about it while I set up the rod."

"Alice!" Doris exclaimed. "You can't climb up on the roof."

"I can so. Come on, Doris, you can help me."

Ellie sank into the chair behind the desk as the two women climbed the stairs, arguing about the lightning rod. She wanted to go home, but she wanted to be alive when she did it. Would this work, or could she get harmed?

"It's okay, Ellie, you can stay with us if you want," Mopsie said, with a wag of her tail.

"Yes," Kitty added, "we wouldn't mind if you stayed. Well, I would, but not the Dumb Dora."

"She's not dumb. And as fond as I've grown of you two in the short time I've been here, I really want to go home to my own talking pets."

"Then you know what you have to do," Kitty said.

Ellie nodded, though the irony didn't escape her either that they needed a lightning bolt with 1.21 gigawatts of power. "Well, it worked for Doc Brown and Marty McFly."

"Who?" Kitty asked.

"Never mind." Ellie rose to stand as the women returned to the basement.

"It's all set," Alice said. "Have you decided?"

Ellie blew out a shaky breath. "I'm going to do it."

Alice's eyes lit up. "Excellent. Let's see if it works. If you hadn't tried it, I would have. But...I'll let you have the first go, since you want to go home."

The scientist crossed to the large pod and unlocked the door. She waved Ellie inside.

Ellie swallowed hard as she ducked and slid into the leather seat. It creaked under her weight.

Alice leaned inside and poked at a typewriter. A paper scrolled past with the words LOCATION: SALEM FALLS.

"Now, input the date it was when you left your time."

Ellie gulped and placed her hands on the keys, typing in the day and year.

"And now, the approximate time."

Ellie typed in the late afternoon time, giving herself a few minutes' leeway from the last time she recalled seeing before she'd left her bed to retrieve the snacks.

Alice blew out a shaky breath. "All right. Now, all we have to do is wait. If we get a strike, I'll close you in, and away you'll go."

Ellie folded her hands in her lap and settled back in the seat. Her heart pounded as she waited. After fifteen minutes, it slowed. Maybe they wouldn't even get a lightning strike.

She drummed her fingers against her thigh, pressing her lips together. A loud crack of thunder shook the house, startling her.

Alice's eyes went wide a moment later. "Power. We've got power!"

"Quickly, close her in!" Doris yelled, hurrying to the contraption and helping Alice push the door closed.

They bolted it shut as electricity sparked inside.

Alice peered in through the glass window on the door. "Good luck, Ellie!"

"Goodbye, Ellie! It was lovely meeting you!" Doris shouted as yellow crackles of electric current spread over the ball's interior.

"Bye, Ellie! We love you!" Mopsie called.

Kitty flicked her tail. "We'll never forget you."

Ellie waved as the contraption started to shake and rumble. She clutched the seat, trying to steady herself as the metal ball rattled around her.

Sparks flew inside of it. A few landed on her skin, shocking her. The electricity grew more violent until a massive bolt built and shot toward her.

The power jolted her, making her hair stand on end as she jiggled in the seat before everything turned black around her.

* * *

Ellie's eyelids fluttered open. She stared up at the ceiling as she blinked a few times to clear her bleary vision. Doris pressed an ice pack against her head.

"She's awake," Chester said.

Doris leaned away, biting her lower lip as she grabbed Ellie's hand.

"How are you feeling?"

"Are you okay, Ellie?" Mopsie asked.

Kitty yawned and stretched a paw across the bed. "At least she's not dead."

Ellie squeezed her eyes closed. They must have brought her back here after the machine failed to work. She probably passed out when that lightning bolt shocked her.

"She okay?" Tommy's southern drawl asked.

"She's not talking yet," Doris answered. "Maybe we should call for an ambulance."

Ellie pressed her hands over her face before she shook her head and grabbed Doris's hand. "No, no, I'm okay. I don't need to go to the hospital."

Doris grinned at her. "Hey, you're back. You sure you're okay? You took a pretty good hit. You were out."

"I know. The lightning just kept building and building. I passed out when it shocked me."

Doris screwed up her face and shot a glance at Chester, then Tommy. He wandered over and wrapped an arm around her shoulders.

Ellie narrowed her eyes at the gesture. "Why are you doing that to her? You're dating Ava."

"Who?" Doris asked.

Ellie knitted her brows and pushed herself up.

"Easy, easy, you took a heck of a spill and hit your head. You were unconscious when I found you at the bottom of the stairs."

"Stairs," Ellie repeated as she stared at the blanket covering her. "I fell down the stairs."

"Yeah, big time. We couldn't get you to wake up. I called Mac, Jake, Rick, everyone. Rick carried you up the stairs. You've been out for a good ten, fifteen minutes."

"Mac, Rick…" Ellie searched the room. "Jake?"

"I'm here," he called from the porch off the room, rising to lean against the door jamb.

"And you're Mia," Ellie said, fixing her gaze on the blonde.

"Of course, I am. Who did you think I was?"

A chuckle escaped Ellie as she rubbed Lola's head. "And Lola and Cleo. Ohhh, I'm so happy to be home."

"Home?" Mia asked. "Ellie, are you okay?"

"Oh, I'm just perfect." She grinned as she let her eyes scan all of her friends. "I just…I had a really weird dream when I was out."

"Dream?" Mac asked. "What kind of dream?"

"I dreamt that I went to nineteen twenty-four. And all of you were there. But you were all different people. Mia, you were a woman named Doris, and you owned the B&B. It was a boarding house then. And you had two pets that looked just like Cleo and Lola."

She pointed to Mac. "And you were the sheriff. Named Chester."

"And Andy was the doctor."

She flicked her gaze to Rick, then Jake. "And you two were mobsters. Tommy Two Toes and Bugsy Malone."

Jake chuckled at the names as he exchanged a glance with Rick while Mac typed on his phone.

"And Scarlett was a woman named Ava. And Hazel was a reporter named Blanche. And Val owned the haunted house on the corner in town. Her name was Flo. And Sam, sweet Sam, she was a scientist named Alice. She helped me come home."

"Wow, you've got quite the imagination," Mia said, with a chuckle.

"Not really," Mac countered.

"What do you mean, Mac?" Rick asked.

"Well, Ellie must have been studying up quite well on the time period to know all those names."

"I haven't been," Ellie said, with a shake of her head.

Mac spun the phone to face the others. "Well, here's Chester, the sheriff in nineteen twenty-four."

Ellie's jaw dropped as she stared at an image that could be Mac.

"And this," he said, with a flick across his screen, "is Alice and Doris."

Mia gasped as she stared at a face much like her own.

Jake approached and squinted at the phone. "Wow, that looks like you."

"And here is Tommy Two Toes and Bugsy Malone," Mac said as he brought up another picture.

Ellie flicked her eyebrows up as she stared at the likeness of Rick and Jake in 1920s finery. A chuckle escaped her.

"Well, it looks like maybe I just had a little adventure in the past."

"I hope you made good use of your time there," Mia said.

"Oh, I did," Ellie said, with a raise of her chin. "I did."

THE END

(Except it's only just the beginning!)

* * *

If you enjoyed this novella, check out all of Ellie's adventures in the Middle Age is Murder Cozy Mysteries, starting with Book 1, Moving is Murder.

OTHER SERIES BY NELLIE H. STEELE

Cozy Mystery Series

Cate Kensie Mysteries
Lily & Cassie by the Sea Mysteries
Pearl Party Mysteries
Middle Age is Murder Cozy Mysteries

Supernatural Suspense/Urban Fantasy

Shadow Slayers Stories
Duchess of Blackmoore Mysteries
Shelving Magic

Adventure

Maggie Edwards Adventures
Clif & Ri on the Sea

Printed in Dunstable, United Kingdom

66625991R00050